D0236733

For Terry - L.M.

OXFORD
UNIVERSITY PRESS

Great Clarendon Street, Oxford OX2 6DP

Oxford University Press is a department of the University of Oxford.
It furthers the University's objective of excellence in research, scholarship,
and education by publishing worldwide in

Oxford New York

Auckland Cape Town Dar es Salaam Hong Kong Karachi
Kuala Lumpur Madrid Melbourne Mexico City Nairobi
New Delhi Shanghai Taipei Toronto

With offices in
Argentina Austria Brazil Chile Czech Republic France Greece
Guatemala Hungary Italy Japan Poland Portugal Singapore
South Korea Switzerland Thailand Turkey Ukraine Vietnam

Text copyright © 2015 Mark Sperring
Illustration copyright © 2015 Layn Marlow

The moral rights of the author and artist have been asserted

Database right Oxford University Press (maker)

First published 2015

All rights reserved. No part of this publication may be reproduced,
stored in a retrieval system, or transmitted, in any form or by any means,
without the prior permission in writing of Oxford University Press,
or as expressly permitted by law, or under terms agreed with the appropriate
reprographics rights organization. Enquiries concerning reproduction
outside the scope of the above should be sent to the Rights Department,
Oxford University Press, at the address above.

You must not circulate this book in any other binding or cover
and you must impose this same condition on any acquirer

British Library Cataloguing in Publication Data available

ISBN: 978-0-19-273864-6 (hardback)
ISBN: 978-0-19-273865-3 (paperback)

10 9 8 7 6 5 4 3 2 1

Printed in China

Paper used in the production of this book is a natural, recyclable product made
from wood grown in sustainable forests. The manufacturing process conforms
to the environmental regulations of the country of origin

I'll Catch You If You Fall

Mark Sperring & Layn Marlow

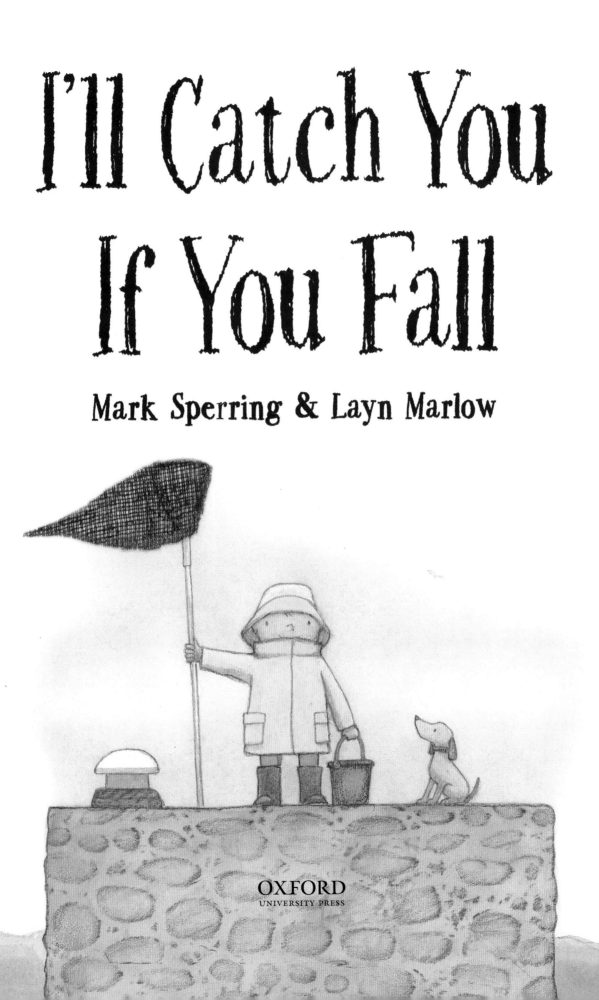

OXFORD
UNIVERSITY PRESS

Who will keep the boy safe?

'I will,' said his mother.

'I will hold him close . . .

'and never let him lean too far,'

But who will keep
them both safe?

'Me,' said the captain.

'I will steer the boat

and keep a watch.'

But who will keep the boat safe?

'I will,'
said the star.

'I will guide the boat
over the foaming waves,

and through the storm . . .

into the little harbour . . .

and all the way home.

But who will keep me safe?'
asked the star.

'I will,' said the boy.

'I will lean out of my window,

but not too far . . .

and

catch

you

if

you

fall.'